Ocean Pearls

A motley assortment of delectable verses

Volume 1

Reena Mahay

Written, compiled and edited by the author.

Ukiyoto Publishing

Dedication

In the loving memory of my dear dad

LATE. MAJOR KUL BHUSHAN MAHAY

(who served the Indian nation in the defence forces
and
allied government services)

Acknowledgement

I would like to express my sincerest gratitude to the God almighty, who has always empowered me with dauntless courage and spirit to tread and carve out novel pathways for myself despite life's odds and challenges which only stoke me at every step to excel more. I truly believe that nothing is possible in this world (at least... no karma) without his acquiescence. For rightly, the **Bhagavad Gita says: Nothing happens without the sanction of God** and we mortals are only instruments of his play and divine drama serving our purpose of birth; enlightening us further on the old verse: "**Karmanye-vadhikaraste Ma Phaleshu Kadachana**". So, I've realized that every step of mine in life is not where I have solely wished to tread, but where he wants to see me going.

And so today, here I am!

I owe a deep sense of gratefulness for whatever miniscule I have grown up to be today - a composite of versatile skills reared over a span of decades - to none other than my family and blessings of my dearest dad from the heaven above. The role of my alma mater and my teachers has nevertheless been instrumental and indispensible - the best educational institutions in the world having been found in the hallowed corridors of Lucknow's convents: St. Agnes' Loreto Day School and Loreto Convent Intermediate College - in instilling in me not only the traits of the head but also of the heart, and also the dogged will not to be deterred from one's values and principles even in this duplicitous world. The immense learning imbibed from here could never be forgotten in life even while functioning with myriad institutions in my learning and teaching career across the length and breadth of the country and even abroad. My salute to my alma mater, as I fondly reminisce my favourite lines from the **Loreto Chorus** thus:

**"Loreto's banner gaily floats
in lands both East and West.**

**Loreto's name each girl reveres
And holds it ever blest."**

Last but not least, I also express my heartfelt gratitude to my friends and well wishers, who I've crossed paths with in my life and they've stood by me in thick and thin. My gratitude to few acquaintances too, who often appear as God's sent angels and infuse in me the vital motivation and inspiration worth emulating. As rightly said, **No man is an island,** so there are many spaces already ventured and many more to be touched further in time, which I look forward to very earnestly, as I consider myself to be a work in progress.

I would also like to thank my publishers and their entire team for their cooperation and support in making this endeavour a global success.

Thank you all.

Preface

Robert Frost has said, **"Poetry is a way of taking life by the throat."**

Do we have the audacity to do it???

Reena Mahay defines a poet thus:

**"A poet is a sculptor –
who chisels raw and rugged pieces
with the right precision of devices;
melody of rhythmic beats or carefree;
and
adorns their structure and form with a figurative sparkle and appeal
to crystallize a palpable sensuous masterpiece for the human senses."**

She puts poetry as…

"Poetry is sprinkling the magic of breath and blood in words by writers with their unique style."

To her a poet rightly stands to be the **first lover of his/her own creation**, akin to Pygmalion falling head over heels for Galatea or a mother sharing an unbreakable bond with her own child.

She believes, **"poetry is a conscious awakening of a distinct insight in each writer which is more a journey inward, an outpour of real emotions, a heartfelt vision, an epiphany"**.

Ocean Pearls is an eclectic collection of few selected poems composed by Reena over the years which have been presented to her readers in this oeuvre as a potpourri of simmering emotions, expressed in diverse poetry forms as a kaleidoscope of assorted, relatable, heartfelt and inspiring perspectives. Each poem breathes different from the other in theme, taste, style and focus, just like each day of life is similar and conspicuously discrete in its flavor and that is what keeps life going with renewed vigor, vitality and hope. The pieces span over themes of mirroring social issues and concerns, existential crisis, dubious social theatrics of masquerading appearances versus reality, nuanced flavors flaunted in embellished relationships and love in today's times, hope to cling to life against all odds, the courage to muster independent critical thought, the grit to find one's own voice amid superimposing mass clamor and bawl, flavors of surrealism, pun and humor, satire, nuances of human behavior and sensibilities, irony, helpless reality gnawing in the face of one's conscience, struggle of humanity and its miseries, apathy and despair, identity versus the weight of arbitrary power and more.

Thus, this esoteric collection gets its name as **'Ocean Pearls'** – the metaphorical 'World' being an ocean and each piece is a chosen pearl selected with utmost precision and treasured as a precious jewel through myriad experiences of life - lived, discovered, witnessed and seemingly oft beyond the apparent - realized. It is noteworthy that most pieces of this anthology have already been published in the literary corridors world-wide.

Contents

A New Dawn

A new twilight, a new spark, a new charm,
a new morrow, a new journey, a new dream
is here,
to set your toe.

Eyes glare yearning with
warm bated breath –
'All' mysteriously gripped in
a budding year's store.

Ushering in promises of
beautiful dawns in tow –
row, row mortals –
row with all your wishful oars.

Float on afloat
as a new leaf born
to glide skies o'er anew
sunrise envisioned...

Hope, Hope, Hope
straddled steadfast –
ride on!
ride on!

Crowning Glory

Rapunzel strong locks —
smart scissors hopped chop...chop...chop...
grasped new skill hands-on!

***haiku**

Metamorphosis

There's much more in this World,
than what our little eyes can detect.

There's much more in this Life,
than what our little minds can comprehend.

There's much more in a 'Human',
than what our tender hearts can decipher or feel.

There's much more in relationships,
than what largely stands conspicuously revealed.

There are more miracles buried in endings,
than what seems predictable to mankind.

The divine orchard is a realm beyond the mind and intellect –
unfathomable, mysterious, mystical – yet sweetly weaned.

Time, itself is a metamorphosis –
with clenched magic, skulking to be unveiled!

A Speck In Eternity

O Time! O Time! O Time!
My lovely Time!
Earnestly long to hop astride your youthful, colossal, adventurous,
enigmatic flaps.
Ah! I'm done with this World!

Aspire to zoom through the foggy lands
And brawny gust - at jet speed
Only to have a sneak peek of what lies there
— Up, Up, Up —

Fly me! Fly me! Fly me!
Above and beyond the beautiful alluring bewitching horizon —
To behold myself awe-struck... at what awaits still
Yet, uncharted in that other Dream World!

— My Speck in Eternity —
I yearn, to witness be!

Change

Don't HOPE for a change;
Don't DREAM for a change;
Don't SCREAM for a change;
Don't WAIT for GODOT's coming!

Hold strong your POWER –
Stand AUDACIOUS –
To SOW and HARVEST –
A desired CHANGE!

Quandary Love

Viscous ooze – surges berserk all night.
Raw green wounds drip red drop-by-drop.
Draped in silence, ache and fright –
Past nightmares hijack my mind.

Balmy consciousness licks and kisses
To bandage my chaste soul –
in vain.

Ah! Have I drowned
In irresistible love
with my excruciating pain?

Skidding Invader

You palm sized, shivering, unwelcomed raider,
how shamelessly you squeezed within...
without a squeak through my window sill.

Made me run around the end of my wits,
as if you're in here on a marathon to hit!

I'll smash you with a racket
and parcel you in a packet!

My, Oh, My!
Your sudden clumsy twists are spectacular seamlessly
to give me unwanted fits!
How perfect to make me trip!

Just you halt:
until my spy Tom traces you for a blind romantic tryst;
sweeps clean a quick master hit;
and enjoys her beloved yummy kill!

Meow!
Meow!

Belch.

Democratic Dandi-Less March*

Cared not for — the proclaimed *lockdown* decree:
more than a thousand miles they trudged barefoot, penniless;
luggage-borne, child-clad, leaderless – towards their dream
destination.

Or the agony, blaze; hunger, thirst;
disease, infection; anxiety, shock;
dreaded plight faced quite uncalled for.

Rights are *rights* –
and its but a choice to relentlessly stand or struggle
for them in mute or in shame.

Oft justice is a prolonged tiresome wait
and its immense suffering to see your brethren yield to dust,
get lashed or go lame.

No wonder some exist out of the game –
never hunger or lust for reign, riches or fame
— if only one thought —

A human is but a *Human* -
A potpourri of flesh, blood, breath and bones,

beyond class, creed, colour, status or name.

TWENTY-Twenty it was — over forty million, *World Bank* held,
Marched silently across *Bharat* with kith-kin intra and inter-state
To ward the noxious *Virus'* gag at bay!

TWENTY-four *hours* a day... *Alas*!
Nation's *drudge*...!
Only to be *Home* — *healthy and safe*???

***acrostic**

Omnipotent Time

Time doesn't time its time
to value Time.
Yet, the worth of people and
situations change with Time.
Ah! If only people knew what lay
draped to unfold
for oneself in Time?

O Time, Time, Time!
On the clock dial as you march
doggedly squeaking
– sealing men's fate –
with
a twittery chime!

Seed

Be a seed —
Wherever life blows you
Rely on your knack to struggle and sprout.
Never take roots among the wrong men,
Nor ever be part of their dark creepy cloud.

Fiendish Escort

O creepy, merciless, fateful, dutiful plunderer of life!
With dark, drowsy, dumb, deadly – dastard intents –
coupled with tiptoed steps – you lurk around invisible.

How stealthily you rob breath from our tubular veins,
leaving our eye-sockets merely one stony-gaze;
Drive one without wings by a noose on their final
flight —
only to be hopelessly dragged to the Gates.
Miles away to some unknown underworld —
no less a wretched south Black Hole.

Never to compassionately revert the captured, innocent,
beautiful, flowering booty.
Callously, you drop behind a corrosive machinery —
beyond worldly repair.

Drenched with teardrops: all adorned to be disposed,
dumped, discarded off;
only to be laid to rest - to one's best!
You shun the rest - with bated breath and pierced holes
in crimson hearts — wounded, bleeding, thumping wild.

What twin enigma of death and dharma* you are —
Lord Yama!
Complex to the core —
undeciphered, unidentifiable, unfathomable,
uncomprehensible, uninvited, unwelcomed.
Alas! What a universal toll!

If only you knew: how absolutely detestable you stand —
how despicable, how callous —
to strike without care or sensitive caution!

How diabolically you dance to your goals,
only to rule, hack and claim
— every earthly soul!

***dharma – moral righteousness**

Worldly Sensibilities

No word, no text,
no ping, no message,
no call, no scream,
nor a sacrificial brief. . .
Is this the way to lay your best –
to rest?

If at all you'd been critically aware:
in a world of fame,
in a world of name,
in a world of game,
in a world of hypocrisy,
in a world of sycophancy,
in a world of betrayal,
in a world of showbiz,
in a world of recognition,
in a world of immense wealth,
...there is a concealed dread...
of reversals unforeseen.

That's a summative human tragedy!

How insensible and clichéd do we teach and preach?
...Ever thought?
Always smile!
Always be positive!
Always be upbeat!
Always be at the treat!
Never cry!
'Hey, be a perfect walkie-talkie facade, Man!'

You rubbed shoulders with no less a million around —
Ah! When your real 'Self' needed one

to lay your heart bare...
none here
to be found!

Ain't this Life?

How apparently worthy and noble one seems after Life!
And now – here...
one beholds some trillion sudden concerned pops around.

Alas!
What human sensibilities to be found!

Sons Of The Soil

Who said rights are granted in blessed charity?

Who said justice always comes by in gift wraps?

Who said empowerment thrives on statutes solely?

Who said the common man – Mr. Nobody – is a mute meek duckling?

Who said indignant voices can be smothered by sheer baits fed piecemeal?

Who said arbitrary power has no end to its sway?

Who said democracy is blindfold allegiance to sceptered rule's halfwit and fancies?

Some ought not forget we're 'Sons of the Soil' –

Our generations are spent in tilling our beloved fructuous soil – to golden oil.

We're 'Sowers'…

We live for our Motherland and its womb;

For it we die!

Fie!

Some ferociously meted misadventures can't tire or douse our relentless breaths.

Some dug us trenches!

Some stirred us to hush with gas shells!

Some brutally overturned us in spite!

Some shoved us as weeds!

Some raked us as pests!

Some puffed fountains of cold cannons!

Some winnowed us with logs!

Some thrashed us as husk!

Some manhandled us as muck!

Some conceived best to bury us – in nonchalance – enough!

Fie! Fie!

We're pullulating 'Seeds'… scrumptious even when fry!

It's time our non-violent, resolved dissent ticking with

Indomitable spirits abound to make you think!

Oh! How our Bapu – the Mahatma – stands tall even today;

Our ever guiding light… in utter despair.

His calm, resistant, not up-in-arms –

Blows, have paved paths uncharted and fruitful orchards
unforeseen.

And here, We – worthy Sons – lie

To follow suit of our Motherland's bequeathed tradition,

To remind some of the diversity, tolerance and integrity of our
Nation.

Fie! Fie! Fie!

Broad Daylight Carnage

Terror...assault...bloodshed...murder...cold-blooded...
Crime!!!

Siren: Siren: Siren:
Police! Police! Police!
Barge in!
Barge in!
Barge in!

Siren:
Who's dead?
Who's dead?
Who's dead?
Body? Body? Body?
Operation Search begins —

Siren:
Oh dear! Oh dear! Oh dear!
Shit! Shit! Shit!
Body here; Body there; Body everywhere?

Siren:
Who else could it be...?
These obnoxious, nocturnal, feelered, brown-black
dark roaches ransacking this lovely bibliophile's book cabinet,
with such a ridiculous wink!

Siren:
Murder weapon? Murder weapon? Murder weapon?
Murder weapon recovered, Sir.....

Siren:
This...
here:
My brand new Crocs, flip-flop!
I love its flip;
I love its flop!
As much as they piss,
none did I miss:
the old granny; nymphs; smart lads;
imagos - giving me the wildest spin!

Siren:
Damn it; Damn it; DAMN
IT!

Siren:
Go home, Cops;
Here, grab a peppermint!

Look and book for despicable tasks...
Said I, with a squint!

Siren: Siren: Siren:
Good luck, next...
from the depth of my heart!

The View From Here

Killer Virus booms:
baneful pain to sweet breathing
solicits God's blessings!

We

Who dares to paint the world – black, brown or white?

Who provokes us to prove or claim ownership rights – of mine
and thine?

Who sarcastically expounds things as good or bad?

Who makes the world happy or sad?

Who chokes thriving opportunities to harbor impoverishment
or propagates servile prosperity?

Who mints social constructs of ethnical and cultural superiority
or inferiority?

Who callously widens the gulf between the haves and have-
nots?

Who segregates us as born natives or natives-not?

Who preferentially beholds us as rare beauty or abhors our ugly
side?

Who thrusts on us partisan respect or scandalous shame and
happens to murder our pride?

Who snobbishly judges us as perfect or grossly flawed?

Who stokes amidst us hate, violence, abuse, dread, distress –
only to leave us appalled?

Who goes about weaving irrational prejudices and biases?

Who disgustingly drives poverty-stricken away from the riches?

Who makes us cheerfully triumph or mercilessly suffer?

Who sieves the living with unwanted bullets or craftily blasts to exterminate humans as mere flesh?

Who adorns their skin with sequined hides – cut in all shapes and size – and proudly flaunts them with no remorse, nor shame?

Who devours others' frailty chopped on plates with clinks of cheers to celebrate their foul games?

Who acknowledges us as angelic saints or fearful fiends?

Who discriminates us as a joyful Kingpin or as sheer miserable underlings?

Who taught us to be oblivious and stand as spineless spectators to watch others' struggle or scream?

Who are bent on creating a world where sycophancy and nepotism reign outrageously supreme?

Who?

Who?

Who?

Do we then, supplicate...

God, bless us all...

to run away. . .

to shun away. . .

or to wade through these?

And there God stands tall:
mute, helpless and amazed — on

Mortals' inhumane tomfoolery!

Fences: No Offences!

O'er fresh, airy, brimming, breathing,

bountiful spaces and landscapes,

massive labyrinths dug.

Risen stone on stone

brick on brick,

loftily erected in numbness.

Gazing ambitiously awe-struck at the twinkling stars,

fixated mutely,

air mortified within their crevices.

Oft, miles-a-run fading at the feet of the horizon!

Bolstering a sense of nook security.

Ownership – an ecstatic breather!

Mended and tinted with a glossy touch on sunny noons,

adorned with batches of proud honour.

Thatched and solidified with brick and mortar.

Their periphery stands a moat so clean.

Spectacular towers seen soaring –

masons rendered Lilliput in colossal wings.

Thou and mine – enough to whine?

I wonder, how visible a laurel they seem?

I wonder, who marvellously they please?

I wonder, how callously they rip apart Mother Earth's bosom?

One hand thumps hard a chest –
One tongue boasts of peace, brotherhood and humanity. . .
Solidarity, oneness, love and kindness overtly galore. . .

Yet, feed manure through the second hand – on
huts in the countryside...
villas in towns...
mansions in states...
palaces in countries...
stretched insatiably sans bounds
etched indelibly invisible –
on bloody crimson hearts
day in and day out!

A second tongue mounts loaded cannons
Trailed with ease overhead –
To inhale the defensive breeze. . .
In the moonlit light
Secure and serene!

If We Ever Meet Again

If we ever meet again!

If we ever meet again
Let's sit under our favorite banyan tree.
Lay bare our hearts in the monsoon drizzle,
Canopied by rainbow umbrellas and steaming cappuccino treat.

If we ever meet again
Let's play carrom on the lush carpeted green,
Akin to child's play in commemoration of our buddy days
And contest to share the booty – a chocolate cake home-made.

If we ever meet again
Let's twist around the old juke box.
Mesmerize in the floating tunes of
Vintage love songs and bask in nostalgic adventures of youthful
days.

If we ever meet again
Let's lie near the sea shore in the moonlight serene,
And with the approaching waves take stock of our impending
plans –
Unfinished work in progress – folded up our sleeves.

If we ever meet again
Let's wipe each other's silent tears,
Hidden from the world for all bygone years.
Draped under an exuberant facade of successful – manhood
dreams.

If we ever meet again!

Silence

Silence has seasons;
but things people choose to say
have concealed reasons.

*** haiku**

Love

Two brutes
accosted;
scorned;
savagely stoned;
bled and bruised;
hand-cuffed;
street arrested —
for Love.

Shoved in —
for a Bible oath
within the bounds of
a licit Church.

The Raven's gavel
rapped...
shush...shush...shush!

'I love Man. I'm innocent.'
Blurted the other, brazenly unsolicited —
'And, this is me, simply a Sapien on a homo-loving spree!'

'In God's faith,
bonded we stand to plead:
Mercy!!!
Let us – friends of Dorothy – go
scot-free.'

Alas!!!

When will Man
break free —
to grow a heart
to love
and
let love,
unbridled???

Irony!!!

In societal relationships:
to love
and
be loved,
one needs to
fit in
— be tamed —
in black and white
molded frames!

Care To Know Me?

Don't ask me...
'What's your name?'
That could be common.

Don't ask me...
'What have you read?'
That's one's interest.

Don't ask me...
'What credentials you possess?'
That's personal choice and hard work.

Don't ask me...
'Which facts you remember?'
That's memory.

Don't ask me...
'What's your religion?'
That's one's faith.

Don't ask me...
'What is your race?'
That's a social construct – stamped on birth.

Don't ask me...
'Who are the big shots you know?'
That's social sway.

Don't ask me...
'Whose company you keep?'
That's friendship.

Don't ask me...
'Where you come from?'

That's nationality.

Don't ask me...
'Who stands by you?'
That's love.

Don't ask me...
'Who betrayed you?'
That's the humbug world.

Don't ask me...
'Who dislikes you?'
That's preference or prejudice.

Don't ask me...
'What's your lineage?'
That's God given.

Don't ask me...
'What enigma you are?'

To know me —
'All learnings congregate to the power of one Life' -
Know my sum...
Know my thoughts — you're done!

Who else could?
My 'thinking' alone defines me —
In absolute!

Dilemma?

My humble apologies;
You know well...
I'm not born to please!

Come on...look at me!
Ain't I a Human...?
You see!

Alas! My every reaction is a spontaneous,
innocent elicitation
to the qualitative stimulus —
I behold and respond!

So, believe them for free —
When they unfold to you clandestinely...
The good, the bad, the ugly or the googly... about me...!

For there may be many undeciphered versions, yet of me...
even for them...to see!
For I'm a blossoming flower, found fondly
unfolding my sagacious petals daily...
in an unknown, uncharted territory!

Now, in this moment —
All that matters is: what your prudent eyes choose —
to see...the best...
in Me!

Ode To Time

O Time!
Time and time again
I discuss you untiringly;
Time and time again
you remind me of how opportunistic to be;
Time and time again
you set a cry for me;
Time and time again
you validate yourself for me;
Time and time again
you teach me immense fecundity!

O Time!
Time and time again
I forget – why do I perceive you as free?
Time and time again
I feel sorry – I squander you recklessly;
Time and time again
I feel – you're running distant from me;
Time and time again
You lag me behind – to reflect on pensively;
Time and time again
I'm appalled – why this happens each day to me!

O Time!
Time and time again
I plan to time you better yet again;
Time and time again
It feels you're dragging me to some destined place;
Time and time again
I regret your lost company;
Time and time again

I long to revive you once again;
Time and time again
I wish – if only I could time the time timed for me in Eternity!

O Time!
Time and time again
You make me count on you annually, monthly, daily – oft by the
moon walk;
Time and time again
I wait for you often so anxiously;
Time and time again
I plan to sincerely walk abreast with you;
Time and time again
I hate to see you compete with me;
Time and time again
I lack the earnestness to keep a close watch on you!

O Time!
Time and time again
I discover time within time as dawn, noon and dusk;
Time and time again
I wonder, where seems your beginning and end in time?
Time and time again
I'm mesmerized by your melodious pace: tick-tock, tick-tock!
Time and time again
your non-stop tireless moves – fail me simply!

Do you ever realize – what a
loving,
beautiful,
inspirational,
bosom-relationship,
I share with you, Time?

With all the guided somersaulting —
You stand a testimonial vision of my journey in Time.

How adroitly you propel me
to leap in time – every milestone of my Life!

Calm Racquets Rock Fair*

Calm racquets rock fair...
Crackers burst bright fiery flare —
Cruel beasts charred mid-air!

***haiku**

Happy Hallowed Halloween!!!

It's Halloween…Aha!
I've got a buzzing bewitching dark schedule up my sleeve…
What a witchy wacky day in deed – nightmarish indeed!

Time ticking to zero in on…
Which mammoth broomstick would I zoom astride on?
Which witch would I choose to be…beautifully unkempt, gory or
Shakespearean – on a prophetic spree?
Which petrifying, inky furry cloak would I rather swathe on;
embellished with a pointed cone;
ushered by a black whiskered feline,
and nails fascinating in hues dreadful and extreme?

Which dastard goblins and phantoms would I befriend
and revel in impish, untamed camaraderie?
Which living world would I witchily bless with my welcomed
witchi-ness?
How witchfully chilling – would I let out a score of screams and
thunderbolt landing screech?
Which shimmering stout cauldron would I simmer in
my miraculously reeking,
obnoxious potion –
with a crescentic grin?

Which luminous crystal ball would I chant my 'Abracadabra' on,
to witness the unfathomable future unforeseen?
Which would I crave covetously: Trick of Satanic surrealism or
a Treat of blood-filled booze – my dire need?
Which spaces on my bizarre bucket list to venture – on my next
eerie adventure?
Which Hecate-like motherly witch do I in awe emulate
unmindfully?
Which mortals worthy on my rolls – to gag their breath,
haunting them tenderly to half-death?

As I whirled merrily around the Blue Moon's blazing beams – all
set on my stick,
I heard the Universe tremor and blast out a scream:
'Wake up my darling, lovely Witch!'
…Thud...
…Ouch…!

Oh dear... Alas!
What an exhilarating yet a spooky vision,
Shattered to blown shard like a popped popcorn, at last.

"Mama, give me my pumpkin cup of red tea, please!"
Boo-boo!

Hallowine hangover is here, indeed!

Voracious Appetites!!!

Logs, Logs, Logs – Nature's offerings abound –

As you subsume to cindery ashes in fiery Mars-like hearth,

We twirl around as ravenous, wild, starry-furry bears!

What a great scrumptious anticipated surprise;

Of a gala banquet in the frosty, dim, sooty darkness of the Sun-
mislaid night!

How tranquil and spotless feels the bone-chilling blanket spread
tight;

As you blaze and rage in sparkles of crackling fireflies!

Each yellowish, butter-soused, roasted moon – smells sweet of
woody-burnt fumes,

Yet, the imperfect rugged size stands the most endeared hunted
prize;

Post life's slog – for a shrunk and vacuumed belly, in awesome
delight!

Tongues wilted and inundated;

Lips cracked and await parted;

Eyes stare wide and glazed;

Minds focussed and directed –

Wondering.....when the steaming, full blown, mellowed moons
would land on to our gluttonous plates.

To douse nature's kindled sinful human pangs, smouldering in our
unappeasable cauldrons!

Ah! The sole grounds of all Earthly-Worldly strife. . .
Voracious Appetites!!!

Envy!*

I see smoke rise high,

I smell the green fumes of burn,

I feel the fierce flames,

I dare not touch the wild blaze –

I sense the reek of mute pain.

***tanka**

Moon-Less Rendezvous!!!

On this very pitch dark ravenous ritualistic Diwali night,
God's new naked Moon coyly hides its illuminant face.
Draped up in our galaxy's seamlessly sealed black tapestry,
invisibly glaring at the luminant glow of earthly mortals'
frolic and festivities galore!

As I oscillate on my swing, pensive at the earsplitting enchantment
of the bombastic night,
incredibly mesmerized by the gleam of an array of my exquisite
moons
romancing and dangling —
aloft from under the portico of my haven,
glowing to subsume the nascent wintry charm.

Ah! The one shimmering in rainbow hues —
stealthily seems to steal my heart out of its cage,
sneaking gaily from the green veil of the lush
vibrant tendrils of loose, lively, juicy vines,
swaying merrily in the raw breeze,
beheld in row,
by the lens of a thousand lit puny sparkling yellow eyes aglow.

Oh, how failingly oft I swivel my starry, lovey-dovey gaze
to grab a glimpse of its face in trance
and then retreating

as if melting at the very thought of being ogled at!

Is this the ecstatic touch of the sensorial embrace of the wind chill
—

Or the awe of a thousand cascading daffodils dancing in streams of
delight
over me —
Or the vibrant moon's magic woven on a dreamy endearing night
—

Or me missing the real blissful spell of beholding in silence a new
moon night —
that tickles every nerve of my soul
with beaming, bountiful,
millions of star-studded dreams
on the dark canvas,
outstretched visibly to the in-fi-nite!

Happy Holy Holi!!!

Smears of blue-yellow here,

And smudges of green-orange there…

Dabs of silvery sparkles on foreheads here,

Complement dull black streaks on cheeks there…

Splash of red fountains gushing here,

Smash of purple bombs thunder there…

Hip-hop tunes rock here,

Roaring disco beats drumming ears there.

Whiffs of marigolds mesmerize here,

Sniffs of rose-petals abound ecstasy there.

Hordes of untamed sapiens dancing drenched,

In epileptic frenzy within homes and streets.

Oh! Some apparitions chasing on four;

Some ghosts racing with their beloved on two hot wheels!

Thunderbolt screams boom on embracing loved ones

Masquerading in colorful shrieks.

Who's this? …Who's that?

Where's mine? …Where's his?

Senses seem to have lost

Their witty discriminatory shine.

Wandering wild, ragged and haggard –

Once a year is our proud privilege, so dear!

We needn't fear!

Mellowing muscles invigorated
By munching sugary 'Gujiyas'
And crunching potato chips –
A flee day – no less a gala banquet
Packed with hilarity!

Oft time ripe for a dynamic 'raas',
As 'Thandai' and 'Bhang' trickle down
The gullet, stirring a whirlpool of stormy
Exhilaration in a sack – so clean.
Frolic and high spirits
Inhaled in and exhaled out –
Not a second at leisure to wrap
The crap of clumsiest clowns.

A festival of colors ushering sunny Spring –
No eyebrow raised on extending a warm
Cuddle beyond caste, color, creed, gender
Or special age. All painted fair with
Arbitrary strokes of rainbow hues
Reflecting 'One' identity of human race –
Like faces; like attire; like greet; like gait.

Hearts, feelings, thoughts throbbing chaste,
The day smells alluring of palatable taste
And memories of – 'Radha Krishna's Leela' –
A transcendental revived soul feast!

Happy Holi is so holy – a celebratory acme of
Sincere devotion to 'Lord Narasimha',
And a picturesque divine scent of love
Etched
On every humane – mind and heart!

Love Archived

No reason for a word between us today!
Twenties have rolled by.
Then – couldn't dream of this day. . .
In ceremonial space, with kith and kin frolicking abound.

Your eyes roll and set on me and mine on you – a helpless stare...
Minds lost in ecstatic past; unfocused on the decorated faces
mirrored at – shoulder's length.
A promise to never meet each other estranged us – once.
Wish, could treasure vows preceding the last.

Recall:
The tip-toed peeps around green shades;
The love letters kissed;
The shy intimacy so cosy;
Free flow of affectionate connection – blossom.

My heart shafts thunderously like a steam engine even today!
Sneaking to pop out of its bonded cage.
If only, If only, today were any different!
Me in your arms forever – Oh! What bliss!
Alas! All a distant dream!

An era of tales to bare...
I wonder –

When and Where?

Only, wet sparkling pearls roll down seamlessly unaware!

Xmas!!!

Christmas spirit like bees swarms —
Santa, Santa, tinsel tweet abounds;
Cakes, wreaths, holly, trees, gifts, greets dong;
Carols, bells, jingles, jangles chime along;
Love, kisses, merriment in Snowman's burg surrounds!

Magician's Wand

How dry, drab, buried, unanimated and wrapped —
Words retire half-dead in a lexicon.
I pity their mute – captive state!
Some proclaim – a lapidary ardently digs his precious stones,
Neatly draws them out of case and starts to whirl.
Perhaps!

Words…a universe of words. . .
Merrily ablaze incessantly in my smoldering heart-h,
As dancing serpents entranced by charmers' musical contours:
Yearning and swirling to break loose;
Rising and falling in cheers and blues;
Stoked by the fountain depth of feels and hues;
To drench my soul — free of its tire!

An avalanche of cascading torrential sensuousness,
Ripe and raw,
Borne from the core: tender and pure.
How dreadful and spellbound they cast a deluge
From the iota stretch of a swollen-vociferous-puking pen.

Characters and psyche mold face, form and shape –
Swordplay duels – colloquial and rhetoric,
Knit a melodramatic bewitching game.

Ah!
Saints, white – I saw spun flat in vain,
As on Earth, they found no hankered fame.

Hoorah!
All stupendous – cherry red – stardom acts got relayed
By the mastermind, mixed, round souls
Gray –
Half-saints: half-devils;
Which side in: which side out;
I bestow to one's heedful thought – let wit not go rot!

Alas!
For oft idioms stand by as my genie… kick me to swirl and relax a
while in the shade.
Ardently, I clutch a quill and
Cast out the diabolic second Mephistopheles, Frankenstein or
Satan – best in spells,
Until they detonate flat,
Slurping up my life-giving ink to the last suck.

Did you exclaim – you get perceptively
Tinted,
Smitten or
Befuddled
By savoring magicians' words?

Yadda, Yadda, Yadda!

Abracadabra!

Heavenly Stars On Earth!

Two little sweet munchkin globular creatures
bright; and full of light!
Temporarily clouded by thick black
hell-like darkness and out of sight!
Oh, what a respite —
to keep the peepers calm in balm
and wonderfully right!

Dark curtains, beautifully rise and fall –
mechanically oft and on – during sunlight!
What useful wipers to keep the screen all bright!
Coating a moist film
for a dash of flash
or a sparkle glisten; for others
to daze awe-struck — all night!

Owning a classic mind of one's own, they
choose to read and decode the world upside down!
Fuelled by tubular nexus thumping regular fluid:
watery cellular; reviving hot – how bright, a cherry red!
Marvellously, fixed well in sockets to charge
indeed – enlightening up each life and day –
what a doorway at large!

The duos keep the company of a blind spot!
Flaunting a black beautiful smaller dot
captured within a lighter dot —
what amazing glassy marbles – fitted in centre spot!

The couple move to and fro;
how about above and below;
right and left; in diagonal twists;
every degree capable of measure
in full flat circle; from their nerves – a point of hook!

They dance together in ball,
their delight makes others standing tall:
quickly fall!

The combo function as breathing cameras hot-shot:
focussing, clicking, shooting, storing,
memorable moments in a row —
with a faithful accomplice – a buddy store well –
brain and memory in tow!
Mostly active and lively – reluctant never to rest
when in their frolicking best!

Alas! When dog-tired and exhausted, they
don't mind to delve in recharging slumber.
In fiery reddish itch, they lose all game —
how sad –
become sore in pain!
Once infuriated, they cast their frenzy and wrath
dramatic: by bulgy swell and outer protrude
strike distanced terror in others —
to flee with fright or to beg refuge!
This – a natural attribute
to keep most unwelcomed, nowhere near,
but at bay – how simply cute!

A fine pair of long and small curled brush
swipe away the rising dust,
and oft sweep off detestable predators
attempting to make them flush!
Oh! How awfully, such dangerous visitors
get stuck,
vandalize and let their cool comfort suck!

When drowned in a dark well of depression
by this callous world;
their secret floodgates – open wide enough!
To inundate nearby dry hillocks;
with crystal-clear pearl drops or run saline rivers,

else splash heart-wrenching oceanic waves –
so many!
These irresistible floods – no less a contagion –
shoot alike emotions in – on looking gazers
by warming their blood
and wounding their tender hearts, enough!

Once in a while – in life,
their courage might give up —
with overload of labour or nature's rub!
They're bundled to the white-clad masked-man's dissection theatre
and tooled and serviced aplenty...
Cataract. Glaucoma. Hyperopia. Myopia. . .
My, Oh, My, such delicate creatures
they feel 'a tear' in pain – unbearable much!

How often, prescribed right —
use both in conjunction to shoot and aim right!
Some call them bright stars,
some call them shiny pearls,
some call them light houses,
some call them nature's lenses,
some – two lighted suns in one!
Their teeny-weeny rods and cones,
and cones and rods,
run their race, like a unicorn!
To their Master, they're very intensely dear —
a pal never apart, visible –
invisibly visible – round the clock!

They raptly fall in love often:
with humans, animals, insects, objects or
nature – superb!
Changing colour, gaze and slants
during courtships enough!
Turn wild in silent stares,
merrily rotate like balls around,
speak in rhymes: when diseased such!

How deep, buoyant, effervescent, supple – a
sheer innocence enough!
Ah! What a heart-throbbing beauty – sparkles like
a pair in love!

Naturally, so pretty to look at —
Oft decorated wild and free:
with artificial brushes;
and black lined borders;
often changing colourful hues
to blue-green-grey with pastel shades –
obviously, never in haste!

Man, Oh, Man! Thou value them as sight!
What a bright magical light – fixed so right?

Aren't they shining and twinkling stars descended
directly from the Heaven above?

My gratitude, Lord – for this amazing gift –
you blessed us all so much, never to thank enough!

What would our beautiful World and Life be without this
spectacular vision —
bestowed by thee!

Life*

Life is beautiful —
with or without some; for each
breath is divine bliss!

***haiku**

Masked World!

O dear! O dear! O dear!
What a dreaded task?
Show me a face without a mask!

In a World —
Where *mask-less* living and *one-faced* bare giving
is no less a baneful strife akin to Covid;

Where *smiles* aren't contagious,
albeit just a cursory, fleeting, artificial taste;

Where *words* are thoroughly muddled
in the puddle of hypocrite idiosyncrasies;

Where *feelings* are ephemeral, as in a cool ball game
– forever rolling and tossing – on a football field;

Where *actions* are fuelled
and propelled by selfish motives,
more so — for egocentric covetous gains.

O dear! O dear! O dear!
What a dreaded task?
Show me a face without a mask!

In a World —
Where *thoughts* belie words exclaimed
and deeds proclaimed, in honey shrouded states
or in clandestine ways;

Where *love* awfully transpires
surreptitiously to perfidy,
in the micro-second bat of an eyelash;

Where *companionship* is merely a transient ecstatic state –
thunderous chuckles and high-fives
flourish in dubiously sycophant ways;

Where *relationships* heartbreakingly ferment sweet-sour
– shun their beauty, grace, magnetism – giving way
to fatigued, burdensome baggage states;

Where *friendships* gaily bubble only in party thunders –
embellished with wine-clinks of resounding cheers
and futile showbiz of mannequin peers.

O dear! O dear! O dear!
What a dreaded task?
Show me a face without a mask!

In a World —
Where ubiquitous *corruption* is an inconspicuous wild Anaconda
– hissing merrily and kissing venomously –
mercilessly reducing those who dare to mare;

Where *nepotism* and *exploitation*
is the blooming sweet scourge of the day –
sweeping oblivious even beneath a microscopic frame;

Where *racism* and *lawlessness*
rule the roost
– let fair seem foul and foul pose fair –
unheard and subdued;

Where *systemic politics* is an alias name
for a polluted, double-clawed, unruly *trade*
of amassed minions' underdog
puppetry fair;

Where the sceptre of *power* and *authority*
is a blatant bizarre game of chess,
checkmating fair play and faculty – for sheer boost of bigotry
and en-slavery.

O dear! O dear! O dear!
What a dreaded task?
Show me a face without a mask!

Wonder *yesterday*, wonder *today*, wonder fantastically *everyday* —
Ain't this – *a World full of dreaded task*?

Contemplating...
If – a *protection* to blissfully *ever last*???

Ode On Poetry

Poetry is wondrous laughter;
poetry is proud cheer.

Poetry is sheer pleasure;
poetry is mere leisure.

Poetry strikingly evokes humour;
poetry tragically provokes tear.

Poetry grabs its hold on past, present and future;
poetry is a characteristic saga of emulative mortals and deities; yet
breathes ubiquitous and immortal for centuries.

Poetry hums like a bee – a honeyed melody of music;
poetry sums an artist's expression – sensual and crystal clear.

Poetry for few is 'Donne is done', for some no more than
plentiful fun;
poetry for others is no less than intellectual pun.

Poetry is like a sweet scented red rose flown by the dove to one's
darling beloved;
poetry is the heightened regret and pine for unrequited love
gifted by the heartless sweetheart.

Poetry weaves its skin silently with some deep musings and
contemplative thoughts;
poetry leaves none without something wise and mindful taught.

Poetry flows profusely when your mind from chores is freed;
poetry blows other's minds with a lovely sumptuous treat.

Poetry is an arrhythmic dance drenched without rain, often a

kinaesthetic break-dance around in pain;
poetry is a flip-flop extravaganza with no explicit gain.

Poetry shapes its form when our bosom skips a heartbeat;
poetry comes in existence when normal isn't the new norm.

Poetry seems a flight of imagination – without wings in vain;
poetry is a creative conversation – when your soul feels the
confessional drain.

Poetry is a revelation of insights – the kind you hadn't ever
blissfully experienced before;
poetry is an enlightenment of invisible perspectives and harsh
realities – concealed from vision like never before.

Poetry is so often a eulogy to celebrate martyrdom – often a
sorrowful elegy for bereft humans guzzled mercilessly by fumes;
poetry is so often a critical glimpse into socio-political
manoeuvrings – as the society pathetically clamours for radical
change.

Poetry is a beautiful enchantress flocking around merrily in ball;
poetry is a dutiful visionary satirizing around one's painful gall.

Poetry makes you visualise a distinctly colourful mesmerizing
rainbow – as if you were colour-blind before;
poetry makes you listen to the shrill cries of innocence – from
distances unfathomable as never before.

Poetry lets you taste the delectable manna of life as a potion
dripping from heaven;
poetry unfolds your life's experiences as nostalgic memories and
valuable gems always kept to the core.

Poetry is an intake of intoxicating opium overflowing fuzzy
feelings out in trance;

poetry is the harmony of words shooting bubbly emotions
around in prance.

Poetry bestows you the power to touch and heal hearts with love
and tender care;
poetry lets you feel the numb sensations tickle your core, wholly
shunned of overt dread.

Poetry makes you live your fantasies and day-dreams – in
narrated knight tales or distant fairy land sails;
poetry helps you nurse oozing wounds of heart, body and mind –
by bonding our souls to Mother Nature and God's paradise.

O Poetry! O Poetry! O Poetry!
You have no gender – no greed;
You have no religion – no breed;
You have no might – no fight;
You have no face – no race;
You have no name – no game.
All you breathe is a timeless mindset
and —
heart-to-heart mindful, sentimental, frontier-less,
universal connection.

Is it any wonder now – how?
Poetry rejuvenates each life worth a while. . .
By splashing missing colour, fragrance, flavour
or the much needed
— spice!

O Christmas! Merry Christmas!*

Hallelu-
jah! An
irresis-
tible
Christ-
mas
spree!
Half the world arises in
glee, singing carols, hugging-kissing
frolic-king and carefree! Festive spirits
abound twirling a merry go round – ring-a-ring-
a-roses – chilling children toss in fancy robes and
forbidden sobs! Dad Mom rummaging past plans, dar-
ning pending chores pegged since long. Back-to-back list-
ings and mall throngs for the best brand goodies to be stac-
ked and stocked! Wishing one and all good tidings at every
step during mass at chiming Church! Trees towering – conif
erous as green 'A's – embellished with balls, streamers, bells
and ornaments. Flashing with rainbow glittering eyes and white
cotton snowflakes, crowned with a divine Star - gigantic shimmering light-house – constant in glare, in holy frosty night and
borealis twilight! Gifts – carefully wrapped under huge trees'
shade adorned with glittering, beautiful braids, holly, ivy and
ribbon bows – colourful and set to be trailed to kith and kin
across the town. Feasts baked, roasted and dished out, taste
buds simmering with slant gazes, puddings garnished with
rosy cherries and lime zest. Aroma gliding and fluttering
gaily on flight afar. Santa! Santa! Puny eyes peep around,
red coats and stockings nearly flood the burg. Tango in
twos and duos fill the crowds, while Santa is said to plant
blessings in twinkling surrounds! Once at home - chirps, glitters
and burps - with the ever so silent, fluffy and smiling 'Snowman': well
fed, muffler necked! At last, the surprising twists to unwrap gifts – in
guffaw and giggles – a treat never to miss! Oh! Wow!
Now, a dream
fulfilled heavenly
doze! Let's snooze,
sealed with a bliss -
kiss! Ho!...Ho!
....Ho!

----

*concrete poem

About the Author

Reena Mahay

Ms. Reena Mahay hails from the city of Lucknow, India. She holds triple Bachelors in Humanities, Law and Education and a Masters degree, with a plethora of other academic certifications to her credit. Professionally, she's been an academician, IBDP English Educator, social worker and a published writer, poet and critic. She is very passionate about teaching and learning English and also writes since her formative years, not to mention her proclivity towards sketching, art/craft, acting, culinary and other creative arts since school days. Her father also wrote poetry in Urdu, though as an amateur. Ocean Pearls is her debut collection of poetry. Many of her writings have already been published in national and internationally acclaimed research and academic journals, literary magazines and anthologies, e-zines, online and offline literary press and websites globally. She is an ardent advocate of free speech and expression. Her versatile and sensitive persona is best drawn towards the socio-cultural concerns and 'ills facing Man' in the current era, which oft become her muse to chart out her perspective from the voice of her pen. She hopes her readers would relish and appreciate the aesthetics of the selected pieces of this anthology.

9 789360 163884